SAM DOWLING

Is a Dublin-born playwright. He has written and produced nearly thirty plays or small-cast versions of classics for Praxis Theatre Laboratory. His subject-matter has ranged from Irish history through the lives of writers and artists to re-working of themes from the Greek myths. His play about the Brontës (co-written with Andrea Bird) has had three productions in Tokyo.

For more detail see listing in playwrights' database at
www.doollee.com

HA ! HA ! HA ! was commissioned by 1157 Performance Group who first performed it on 10 May 2005 at Norden Farm Centre for the Arts in Maidenhead, Berkshire, with this cast:

NOEL COWARD ....Kevin Johnson

LAURENCE OLIVIER .... Matthew Scott

VIVIEN LEIGH .... Jo Dagless

LUCIA ....Natalie Childs

The production was conceived, designed and directed by Jo Dagless and Matthew Scott, with other texts and films by 1157.

1157 was founded in 1995 by performers Jo Dagless and Matthew Scott, creating a substantial body of idiosyncratic work that fearlessly fuses text, biography, sound, light, image and movement. They have toured widely throughout the U.K. and Ireland from their base as resident theatre company at Norden Farm Centre for the Arts.

IRISH PLAYS AND OTHERS BY SAM DOWLING
IN PRINT AT WWW.LULU.COM OR IN THE PIPELINE

RIVERMAN [Walter Greaves, naïf painter, rise and fall.]
CAULDRON OF BRONTËS [Genius siblings.]
A SEASON IN HELL [Wild poets Rimbaud and Verlaine.]
MOUNTAIN [Life-changing encounters]
RENEWAL [Site-specific version of MOUNTAIN]
TROJAN WOMEN
BIRTH OF THE BEAST [Northern Ireland.]
BIG FELLA! [Michael Collins.]
ALLEGIANCE [IRA in London.]
ANTIGONE
THE FLAME AND THE STONE [Yeats and Maud Gonne.]
VIRGIN OF NOTTING HILL [Sexual problems.]
ORESTEIAN TRILOGY
LOVELOST [Abuse]
RED COUNTESS GREEN CROW [Markievicz and O'Casey]
HA! HA! HA! [Improvisations on Coward and Shakespeare.]

AND SMALL-CAST VERSIONS OF THESE CLASSICS;

THE CENCI
IMPORTANCE OF BEING EARNEST
CHERRY ORCHARD
THREE SISTERS
HEDDA GABLER
WHEN WE DEAD AWAKEN
HAMLET
MACBETH
ANTONY AND CLEOPATRA
THE TEMPEST

IRISH PLAYS AND OTHERS Vol. 19

HA ! HA ! HA !

IMPROVISATIONS AND PARODY
ON
SCENES FROM SHAKESPEARE AND COWARD

by
Sam Dowling

2004-2005

Sam Dowling
85 Haddo House
Haddo Street
LONDON SE10 9SE

praxis.lab@ntlworld.com

Published by Lulu 2007

www.lulu.com

ISBN 978-1-84799-406-6

HA HA HA

Characters

LARRY

LUCIA

NOEL

VIV

Scenes

Scene One	*Twelfth Night* Act 3 Scene 1
Scene Two	*Romeo and Juliet* Act 3 Scene 5
Scene Three	*Private Lives* Act 1
Scene Four	The same
Scene Five	The same
Scene Six	*As You Like It,* Act 5 Scene 2, Sonnet 18 and *Mad Gods And Englishmen*
Scene Seven	*Hamlet* Act 3 Scene 1
Scene Eight	*Hamlet* Act 4 Scene 5
Scene Nine	Anecdotal
Scene Ten	*Macbeth* Act 2 Scene 2
Scene Eleven	*Blithe Spirit* Act 3

THE SCENES are the building blocks for a theatrical event

HA HA 1

[VIV and LUCIA forward.
LUCIA dresses as a man.]

LUCIA
Most excellent and accomplished lady
The heavens rain odours on you !
My matter hath no voice, lady, but to your
Own most pregnant and vouchsafed ear

OLIVIA
Let the garden door be shut, and leave me
To my hearing.
Give me your hand, sir

LUCIA
My duty, madam, and most humble service

VIV
What is your name ?

LUCIA
Cesario is your servant's name, fair Princess

VIV
My servant, sir ! 'Twas never merry world
Since lowly feigning was called compliment.
Y'are servant to the Count Orsino, youth.

LUCIA
And he is yours, and his must needs be yours.

Your servant's servant is your servant, madam.

VIV
For him, I think not on him, for his thoughts,
Would they were blanks rather than filled with me!

LUCIA
Madam, I come to whet your gentle thoughts
On his behalf

VIV
O, by your leave, I pray you:
I bade you never speak again of him;
But, would you undertake another suit,
I had rather hear you to solicit that
Than music from the spheres.

LUCIA
Dear lady-

VIV
Give me leave, beseech you. I did send,
After the last enchantment you did here,
A ring in chase of you; so did I abuse
Myself, my servant, and, I fear, you.
Under your hard construction must I sit,
To force that on you in a shameful cunning
Which you knew none of yours. What might you think ?
Have you not set mine honour at the stake
And baited it with all the unmuzzled thoughts
That tyrannous heart can think ? To one of your receiving
Enough is shown, a cypress, not a bosom,

Hides my heart. So let me hear you speak.

LUCIA
I pity you

VIV
That's a degree to love

LUCIA
No, not a grize; for 'tis a vulgar proof
That very oft we pity enemies

VIV
Why then, methinks 'tis time to smile again.
O world, how apt the poor are to be proud !
If one should be a prey, how much the better
To fall before the lion than the wolf !
.....
The clock upbraids me with the waste of time.
Be not afraid, good youth, I will not have you.
And yet, when wit and youth have come to harvest,
Your wife is like to reap a proper man.
There lies your way, due west.

LUCIA
Then westward-ho!
Grace and good disposition attend your ladyship !
You'll nothing, madam, to my lord by me ?

VI
Stay.
I prithee tell me what thou think'st of me.

LUCIA
That you do think you are not what you are.

VIV
If I think so, I think the same of you.

LUCIA
Then think you right: I am not what I am.

VIV
I would you were as I would have you be !

LUCIA
Would it be better, madam, than I am ?
I wish it might, for now I am your fool.

VIV
O, what a deal of scorn looks beautiful
In the contempt and anger of his lip !
A murd'rous guilt shows not itself more soon
Than love that would seem hid: loves' night is noon.
Cesaraio, by the roses of the spring,
By maidhood, honour, truth, and everything,
I love thee so that, maugre all thy pride,
Nor wit, nor reason can my passion hide.
Do not extort thy reasons from this clause,
But rather reason thus with reason fetter;
Love sought is good, but given unsought is better.

LUCIA
By innocence I swear, and by my youth,
I have one heart, one bosom, and one truth,
And that no woman has, nor never none
Shall mistress be of it, save I alone.
And so adieu, good madam, never more
Will I my master's tears to you deplore.

VIV
Yet come again, for thou perhaps mayst move
That heart which now abhors, to like his love.
....
Here, wear this jewel for me; 'tis my picture.
Refuse it not; it hath no tongue to vex you.
And I beseech you come again tomorrow.
What shall you ask of me that I'll deny,
That honour sav'd may upon asking give ?

LUCIA
Nothing but this... your true love for my master.

VIV
How with mine honour may I give him that
Which I have given to you ?

LUCIA
I will acquit you.

VIV
Well, come again to-morrow. Fare thee well,
A fiend like thee might bear my soul to hell.

LUCIA
'You think you are not what you are...'
I don't know what he means

VIV
She's a beautiful rich and powerful woman behaving like a tart

LUCIA
Isn't that what beautiful rich and powerful women do ?

VIV
You think I behave like a tart

LUCIA
A bit

VIV
You despise me

LUCIA
I love you

VIV
'I have one heart...
No woman will be mistress of it...'

LUCIA
But every man

VIV
Every man I meet tries to seduce me
Which is quite another matter
Sometimes I say yes
Sometimes maybe

LUCIA
Never no

VIV
No is so negative

LUCIA
As a photographer the negative is part of my creative process

VIV
That's why photography will always be a minor art
The great actor says yes to everything

LUCIA
Not to torture...abuse..m..

VIV
Yes to torture and abuse because they happen

LUCIA
I have to say no to murder

VIV
I say yes to murder because murder is done by humans like me

I could murder

LUCIA
You could not

VIV
I'm warning you I'm dangerous !
Lucky for you I don't murder my friends
I remember my opening night as Lady Macbeth... just before going on stage
I glanced in my dressing mirror
This monster of a woman looked out at me... straight in the eye
As she settled a stray hair over her ear
It taught me a lesson about looking in mirrors

LUCIA
Still you think you are not what you are

VIV
I am not yet what I may become

LUCIA
An Olivier

VIV
A Bernhart

LUCIA
You backed off love for another woman in that scene

VIV
That was about Larry and me
Every love-scene I do.... with you or anyone else
Is really with Larry
He is the mediator of my entire sexual and emotional life
That may be a strength or a weakness
But it's a fact and I have to live with it
It represents quite an output believe me

LUCIA
Lucky old you

VIV
When Larry and I are together we just fuck and fuck and fuck

LUCIA
Lucky old Larry

VIV
You know something Lucia ? It still isn't enough for him
I'm terrified to let him out of my sight
Do you know where he is right now ?

LUCIA
I think he's working on a song with Noel

VIV
If you see anything betwen them
You have to let me know right away

LUCIA
I won't spy on him Viv
No more than I'd spy on you

VIV
You're my friend, Lucia... you have to protect me

LUCIA
I'll fight demons for you Viv
But I'll not play the spy

VIV
What kind of friend is that !

HA HA 2

LARRY
I'm off darling

VIV
Don't go

LARRY
I must

VIV
I need you

LARRY
I'm meeting John to work on Scene One
O! I am Fortune's fool

VIV
Wilt thou be gone ? It is not yet near day
It was the nightingale and not the lark,
That pierced the fearful hollow of thine ear.
Nightly she sings in yonder pomegranate tree.
Believe me love, it was the nightingale.

LARRY
It was the lark, the herald of the morn,
No nightingale: look, love, what envious streaks
Do lace the severing clouds in yonder east:
Night's candles are burnt out, and jocund day
Stands tiptoe on the misty mountain tops:
I must be gone and live, or stay and die.

VIV
Yon light is not daylight, I know it, I;
It is some meteor that the sun exhales,
To be to you this night a torch-bearer,
And light thee on thy way to Mantua.
Therefore stay yet: thou needs't not to be gone

LARRY
Let me be ta'en, let me be put to death;
I am content, so thou wilt have it so.
I'll say yon grey is not the morning's eyes,
'Tis but a pale reflex of Cynthia's brow,
Nor that is not the lark, whose notes do beat
The vaulty heaven so high above our heads:
I have more care to stay than will to go:
Come death and welcome ! Juliet wills it so.
How is't, my soul ? let's talk; it is not day.

VIV
It is, it is; hie hence, be gone, away !
It is the lark that sings so out of tune,
Straining harsh discords and unpleasing sharps.
Some say the lark makes sweet division,
This does not so, for she divideth us;
Some say the lark and loathed toad change eyes;
O! now I would they had changed voices too,
Since arm from arm that voice doth us affray.
O! now begone; more light and light it grows.

LARRY
More light and light; more dark and dark our woes.

VOICE
The day is broke; be wary, look about.

VIV
Then, window, let day in, and let life out.

LARRY
Farewell, farewell ! one kiss, and I'll descend.

VIV
Art thou gone so ? my lord, my love, my friend !
I must hear from thee every day in the hour,
For in the minute there are many days:
O! by this count I shall be much in years
Ere I again behold my Romeo.

LARRY
Farewell !
I will omit no opportunity
That may convey my greetings, love, to thee.

VIV
O! think'st thou we shall ever meet again ?

LARRY
I doubt it not; and all these woes shall serve
For sweet discourse in our time to come.

VIV
O God ! I have an ill-divining soul:
Methinks I see thee, now thou art so low,

As one dead in the bottom of a tomb:
Either my eyesight fails, or thou look'st pale.

LARRY
And trust me, love, in my eye so do you;
Dry sorrow drinks our blood. Adieu ! Adieu !

[Exit]

VIV
O fortune, fortune ! all men call thee fickle:
If thou art fickle, what dost thou with him
That is renown'd for faith ? Be fickle, fortune;
For then I hope, thou wilt not keep him long,
But send him back.

[Re-enter LARRY.]

LARRY
Ho ! daughter, are you up ?

[Embrace.]

VIV
Larry, I can't face the day without you

LARRY
Come with me

VIV
Am I unnatural ?
I want to eat you

LARRY
You're a bit scary

VIV
I need your sex every day in the hour

LARRY
We have to work

VIV
It's part of the work... like coffee-breaks
Larry, the work was never better

LARRY
You'll wear me out

,,,,,
What is it ?

VIV
You're fucking someone else !

LARRY
How the fuck could I find the energy to fuck someone else ?

VIV
Who is she ? I'll kill you both !

LARRY
There is no other she

VIV
A man ! Who is he ?

LARRY
No he no she but thee !

VIV
Noel !

LARRY
I can't be late for Gielgud

VIV
Fuck Gielgud and if you do I'll kill you both
And never play my Juliet
Hie hence, be gone, away !
O ! now be gone.

HA HA 3

[LUCIA & NOEL forward.
VIV and LARRY withdrawn.]

NOEL
Not a bad view

LUCIA
It's breathtaking !
Oh Darling..... I'm so happy

NOEL
Are you ?

LUCIA
Aren't you ?

NOEL
Naturally... frightfully happy

LUCIA
Can you believe it ?
Man and wife

NOEL
Indeed

LUCIA
Don't laugh
Remember this is my first
Kiss the bride

NOEL
(Kiss) There

LUCIA
Properly

NOEL
(Kiss) That better ?

LUCIA
Three for luck

NOEL
(Kiss) Pet

LUCIA
Are you glad you married me ?

NOEL
Obviously

LUCIA
How much glad ?

NOEL
Unbelievably glad

LUCIA
That's nice
Gladder than last time ?

NOEL
Don't keep on about last time

LUCIA
I won't
Was she absolutely beautiful ?

NOEL
Terribly

LUCIA
More beautiful than me ?

NOEL
Oh yes

LUCIA
Darling !

NOEL
Sophisticated and svelt and smooth and strong and soft...

LUCIA
Could she map-read like me ?

NOEL
She couldn't read a map to save her life

LUCIA
Aha !
Did she have my way with horses ?

NOEL
No and she didn't have your wayward mother

LUCIA
You don't like my mother
She's quite sweet underneath

NOEL
I didn't look underneath
You married me to escape from her

LUCIA
I married you because I love you

NOEL
Oh dear me !
I married you to be safe and warm and unbruised
You're going to find me awfully boring

LUCIA
You couldn't be boring if you tried

NOEL
You're going to understand me perfectly...

LUCIA
I'll try

NOEL
...So you can manipulate me

LUCIA
This guy is a real shit
I mean what did he marry the poor girl for?

NOEL
To be safe and warm and unbruised

LUCIA
He's gone and married his mother

NOEL
I'm afraid he's gone and married her mother
He'll see when he gets underneath

LUCIA
But he doesn't

NOEL
Does he not ?

LUCIA
You wrote it

NOEL
I haven't read it

LUCIA
Be serious

NOEL
Never

LUCIA
Never ever ?

NOEL
Well...always
Making fun of mankind is a serious business

LUCIA
Do you mind me photographing you ?

NOEL
I love it
Make sure you get my good side

LUCIA
Is that the inside or the outside ?

NOEL
Inside

LUCIA
That takes longer

NOEL
I'm not given to introspection

LUCIA
....

NOEL
You don't like that

LUCIA
I accept what's given
Surface or the slippery stuff

NOEL
I confess to be what I appear to be

LUCIA
Successful writer

NOEL
Guilty m'lud

LUCIA
Composer

NOEL
Of ephemera

LUCIA
Actor

NOEL
Clown

LUCIA
That too
Handsome

NOEL
Modesty forbids...

LUCIA
Thief…

NOEL
Never
I borrowed one joke from Oscar Wide

LUCIA
Thief of a thousand women's hearts

NOEL
All freely given
I confess to nine hundred and ninety-nine
Who ever could you be thinking of for the other one ?

LUCIA
Rich

NOEL
Driven into tax-exile
To salvage a few coppers for my old age
I am officially resident in Bermuda
Though I live in Jamaica
I earn my crust in the United States
And hold subsidiary residency in Switzerland
Where I have a small villa, a large dog
A silent banker and a clever accountant
Above all I remain the most British and loyal of royalists
I believe in the Windsors as others believe in the Blessed Trinity
Rather more in fact since they sometimes invite me to dinner

And very occasionally to bed

LUCIA
The Blessed Trinity

NOEL
They are simply divine

HA HA 4

[VIV and NOEL forward on adjoining balconies.
Unseen by each other they sit back to back
taking in the pleasant view.
MUSIC starts up below... a sentimental melody.
Both react strongly to it.
NOEL hums along. VIV, shocked, hears and recognises him.
She takes up the tune until the equally shocked NOEL
hears then sees her. They stand and face each other.]

VIV
It wasn't me [...the music]

NOEL
I wouldn't put it past you

VIV
Are you spying on me ?

NOEL
I'm on my honeymoon

VIV
Hah !
You said you'd never marry again

NOEL
Are you spying on my honeymoon ?

VIV
I'm on mine

NOEL
Oh very nice
Better this time ?

VIV
Much
Actually it hasn't really started

NOEL
Me too

VIV
Well...have a happy marriage

NOEL
And many happy returns
See you around

VIV
I could do without ever seeing you again this side of Hell

NOEL
I look forward to seeing you there

VIV & NOEL
Good-bye

[Withdraw.]

HA HA 5

[Enter LARRY]

NOEL
You be him for a bit

LARRY
Where's the script ?

NOEL
We're just improvising
I'll be in the lounge

[Withdraws.
LUCIA is weeping.]

LARRY
If you don't stop caterwauling I'll break your neck !

LUCIA
You're a beast ! Beast ! Beast !
Oh Mummy ! Mummy ! Mummy !

[Withdraws.
VIV forward.]

LARRY & VIV
I need a drink
.......?

LARRY & VIV
There's drink here
...... ?

LARRY & VIV
I'm so angry !
........?

LARRY
Whose is the big yacht ?

VIV
The Onassis crowd usually

LARRY
I wish I were on it

VIV
I wish you were on it

LARRY
Don't try to be smart

VIV
I most certainly shall

LARRY
If you push me I swear I'll kill you !

VIV
You've tried it often enough

LARRY
From the cursed moment you entered my life
It's been nothing but misery

VIV
Oh shut up !

LARY
There's no end to it
You brought a curse on my very existence

VIV
Let's have another

LARRY
Right
Ice ?

VIV
We could get paralytic drunk

LARRY
It didn't work in Venice

VIV
It nearly worked in Paris

LARRY
Everything nearly works in Paris

VIV
Here's mud in your eye

LARRY
In yours
You in love with him ?

VIV
Naturally

You in love with her ?

LARRY
Naturally

LARRY & VIV
There you go
... ?

VIV
What's she like ?
Apart from the caterwauling ?

LARRY
Lovely...innocent... intelligent... widely read... sporting.. knows horses...reads maps a treat...

VIV
How innocent ?

LARRY
Perfectly
What's yours like ?

VIV
None of your business

LARRY
No need to tell him I'm here

VIV
I told him

LARRY
Discreet as ever

VIV
Don't fret... he won't hurt you

LARRY
If he lays a finger on me I'll scream the house down

VIV
Does yours know I'm here ?

LARRY
No
I tried to get her to leave

VIV & LARRY
He [She] won't budge
...?

[Sentimental music}

LARRY
That must be the fifth time they've played that soppy tune

[BOTH might hum or sing-along]

....
......

VIV
I'm really sorry about all this

LARRY
Me too
...
Just my luck

VIV
I promise I'll leave in the morning

LARRY
You're really very kind
....
You deserve to be happy this time

VIV
You too
....

LARRY
Such rubbish

VIV
Funny the way rubbishy music plays tricks with memory

LARRY
What were you remembering ?

VIV
I went to see you in the Theatre Royal
Every night for a month
I'm going to marry that man, I said to my friend
He's married and so are you
I don't care

LARRY
You crept into my crowded dressing-room
Like a shaft of sunlight on a Winter's day

VIV
I had to come in to say I think you're marvelous

LARRY
You kissed me lightly on the shoulder as you left
I couldn't move my arm for half an hour...

VIV
Frightening...

LARRY
...Or wouldn't

VIV
...How much I still love you

LARRY
It's the only thing that matters to me now

VIV
Lock the door

LARRY
I don't think I can

VIV
Lock the door and we'll see

LARRY
There's no key

VIV
Come here my love

LARRY
They'll be back any minute

VIV
Nice surprise for them

LARRY
You're a shameless hussy

VIV
You are insatiable

LARRY
You'll wear me out

VIV
Does Hamlet steal Ophelia's virginity ?

LARRY
Probably

VIV
I want to play Ophelia

LARRY
I'll see what I can do

HA HA 6

[LUCIA disguises herself as a man]

NOEL
We're in the Forest of Arden
I'm Orlando... on the run from a cruel brother
Madly in love with Rosalind

LUCIA
And I with Orlando
Because I'm on the run from a wicked uncle
I'm disguised as a man, Ganymede

VIV
I'm madly in love with Ganymede

LARRY
I'm madly in love with Phebe

[LUCIA and NOEL forward.]

LUCIA
...Believe then, if you please, that I can do strange things.
I have, since I was three years old
Convers'd with a magician
Most profound in his art and yet not damnable.
If you do love Rosalind so near your heart as your gesture cries it out,
when your brother marries Aliena shall you marry her. I know not into what
straits of fortune she is driven, and it is not impossible to me, if it appear not inconvenient to you, to set her before your eyes to-morrow, human as she is, and without any danger.

NOEL
Speak'st thou in sober meanings ?

LUCIA
By my life, I do; which I tender dearly, though I say I am a magician. Therefore
put you in your best array, bid your friends; for if you will be married to-morrow, you shall, and to Rosalind, if you will.

[VIV and LARRY forward.]

Look, here comes a lover of mine, and a lover of hers.

VIV
Youth, you have done me much ungentleness
To show the letter that I writ to you.

LUCIA
I care not if I have. It is my study
To seem despiteful and ungentle to you.
You are there follow'd by a faithful shepherd;
Look upon him, love him, he worships you

VIV
Good shepherd, tell this youth what 'tis to love.

LARRY
'Tis to be all made of sighs and tears;
And so am I for Phebe.

VIV
And I for Ganymede.

NOEL
And I for Rosalind.

LUCIA
And I for no woman

LARRY
'Tis to be all made of faith and service;
And so am I for Phebe.

VIV
And I for Ganymede

NOEL
And I for Rosalind

LUCIA
And I for no woman

LARRY
It is to be all made of fantasy,
All made of passion, all made of wishes,
All adoration, duty, and observance,
All humbleness, all patience, all impatience,
All purity, all trial, all obedience,
And so am I for Phebe.

VIV
And so am I for Ganymede.

NOEL
And so am I for Rosalind.

LUCIA
And so am I for no woman.

VIV
If this be so, why blame you me to love you ?

LARRY
If this be so, why blame you me to love you ?

NOEL
If this be so, why blame you me to love you ?

LUCIA
Why do you speak too, "Why blame you me to love you ?"

NOEL
To her that is not here, nor doth not hear

LUCIA
I pray you, no more of this; 'tis like the howling of Irish wolves against the moon.
[To LARRY] I will help you if I can.
[To VIV] I would love you if I could.
To-morrow meet we all together.
[To VIV] I will marry you if I ever marry woman, and I'll be married to-morrow.
[To NOEL] I will satisfy you if I ever satisfied man, and you shall be married to-morrow.

[To LARRY] I will content you if what pleases you contents you, and you shall be married to-morrow.
[To NOEL] As you love Rosalind, meet.
[To LARRY] As you love Phebe, meet; -and as I love no woman, I'll meet.
So, fare you well; I have left you commands.

LARRY
I'll not fail, if I live

VIV
Nor I

NOEL
Nor I
......
......
Actually my character.... What do they call him ? ....
Orlando
Has rather fallen for you as the man, Ganymede
Though I, the actor, know you're a woman playing a woman disguised as a man

LUCIA
You're not playing the script

LARRY
Love is all fantasy

VIV
Love is all chemistry

LUCIA
There's nothing in the script to suggest Orlando fancies Ganymede

NOEL
There is for me
Maybe not for another actor

VIV
A powerful chemistry is activated when Rosalind meets Orlando
Surely that turns on again when they meet and she's disguised as a man

LARRY
Fantasy turns it off double-quick
'I don't want to love a man'

NOEL
No
Fantasy says 'I fear loving a man'

VIV
I'm really lucky
Women don't turn me on sexually

LUCIA
You turn me on sexually

VIV
....
I don't know what to say about that

It's kind of flattering
But I hope you don't expect me to explore the possibilities

LUCIA
That's your decision

VIV
You wouldn't rape me

LUCIA
That's right

VIV
Thank you
Or make a pass at me

LUCIA
Give me credit for some subtlety

VIV
I'm afraid if I fancied you I'd make a pass at you

LUCIA
I'll live in hope then

VIV
Not anticipation dear

LUCIA
I can't help being an optimist

VIV
I really love you Lucia
But the thought of having sex with you is obscene

LUCIA
Ouch !
And with Larry ?

VIV
Warming as the prospect of a hot dinner

LUCIA
And with Noel ?

VIV
I count you as a real friend, Noel
……
There's nothing sexual in it… is there ?
Though I know you're the great ladies' man

LUCIA
The men are silent on the subject
……
……
……

NOEL
I'm a prude
…..
I don't know where I got the name of being a ladies' man
I never looked for it

LUCIA
You love women

NOEL
Not when they go all laddish
Dress like out-of-work pot-holers
Swearing and boozing

VIV
I like swearing
I like boozing
I like clothes that let me sprawl

NOEL
It will be the end of womanhood

LUCIA
You don't want womanhood
You want a world of dolls in fancy-dress
Non-swearing non-shitting porcelain dolls

NOEL
Lovely women don't shit

VIV
Or fuck

NOEL
Of course not

LUCIA
I see why women love you

You put them on a pedestal

NOEL
You put them on a toilet-bowl
If my life and work are about anything
It's attempting to bring a little joy and beauty
Into a world sinking into crassness posing as talent
Mediocrity marketed as celebrity

VIV
I need love in my world

NOEL
Love ?
I love the sound of laughter
In the theatre or the living-room
I worship beauty restraint and intelligence

LUCIA
You have no hate in you

NOEL
Hate is too strong a word
I have aversions you could count in legions
Pornography... it bores me
Squalor terrifies me
I would willingly let the Government take half my exiled wealth
If I were sure it would eliminate pornography and poverty
Or even if they would spend it on beautiful things

VIV
Who would decide what is beautiful ?

NOEL
We would
.....

' Shall I compare thee to a Summer's day ?
Thou art more lovely and more temperate.
Rough winds do shake the darling buds of May,
And Summer's lease hath all too short a date;
Sometimes too hot the eye of heaven shines,
And often is his gold complexion dimm'd;
And every fair some times from fair declines,
By chance, or nature's changing course, untrimm'd;
But thy eternal summer shall not fade
Nor lose possession of that fair thou ow'st;
Nor shall Death brag thou wand'rest in his shade,
When in eternal lines to time thou grow'st.
So long as men can breathe or eyes can see,
So long lives this, and this gives life to thee. '

.....
I'd give the other half of my exiled wealth
To have written that

LUCIA
You seemed to deliver it to Larry

NOEL
He was being left out of things

LARRY
I like listening... sometimes

VIV
It's obviously meant for a woman

NOEL
It doesn't matter

VIV
It matters to me
I found it offensive
Remember you're in my house

NOEL
You're my best friends

VIV
Don't try to come between me and Larry
It's not the first time is it Lucia ?

LUCIA
Aw Viv !

VIV
And the same goes for you
And all the arse-lickers that try to muscle in on our relationship
....
.....
Have you nothing to say Larry ?

LARRY
....

....

Ice in the gin everyone ?

......

......

[The silence is broken by infectious laughter.
NOEL and LARRY sing *Mad Gods and Englishmen*]

NOEL and LARRY

In the torrid zones where the English holiday
Native carpet sellers tire
When the sun beats down like fire
Comes the moment when the masses melt away
Every local takes siesta
In the steaming heat to rest an hour or two

Tossapenny tossapenny tossapenny tosh !
Tossapenny tossapenny tossapenny tosh !
Ginantonic ginantonic ginantonic gosh !
Ginantonic ginantonic ginantonic gosh !

The indigenous bunch eat a hearty lunch and bee-line for the bed
But the Brits go out to take the sun instead

Mad gods and Englishmen
Go out in the midday sun
Egyptians ain't inclined to
The Greeks are too refined to
Serbs and Croats snooze in peace from twelve to two
But your Brit is not inclined to recline too
On the upper Nile
All rest a while
To avoid the dreaded heat
In the Phillipines
By every means
They avoid the scorching street
As noonday tolls
Every shop will close
And the locals cut and run
But mad gods and Englishmen
Go out in the midday sun

HA HA 7

[NOEL and LUCIA, VIV and LARRY, in two concurrent dialogues.]

NOEL
Soft you now !
The fair Ophelia ! Nymph, in thy orisons
Be all my sins remembr'd.

VIV
He doesn't make love to me any more.

LUCIA
Good my lord,
How does your honour for this many a day ?

VIV
Why don't you fuck me any more, Larry ?

NOEL
I humbly thank you; well, well, well.

LARRY
You mean why haven't I fucked you in the last hour

VIV
Yes

LUCIA
My lord, I have remembrances of yours,
That I have longed to re-deliver;

I pray you, now receive them.

VIV
You promised we'd make love till hell froze over

NOEL
No not I;
I never gave thee aught

LUCIA
My honoured lord, you know right well you did;
And, with them, words of so sweet breath compos'd
As made the things more rich: their perfume lost,
Take these again; for to the noble mind
Rich gifts wax poor when givers prove unkind.
There, my lord..

LARRY
We were two love-struck kids

VIV
I was a child
You were a mature man

NOEL
Ha ha ! Are you honest ?

LUCIA
My lord !

LARRY
Oh Lord !

NOEL
Are you fair ?

LUCIA
What means your lordship ?

NOEL
That if you be honest and fair, your honesty should admit no discourse to your beauty.

VIV
Other men still find me attractive

LUCIA
Could honesty, my lord, have better commerce than with beauty ?

LARRY
Other men still find me attractive

NOEL
Aye truly; for the power of beauty will sooner transform honesty from what it is to a bawd than the force of honesty can translate beauty into its likeness; this was sometime a paradox, but now the time gives it proof. I did love thee once.

LUCIA
Indeed, my lord, you made me believe so.

LARRY
I love you as much as ever

VIV
Liar !

NOEL
You should not have believed me; for virtue cannot so inoculate our old stock but we shall relish of it: I loved you not.

LARRY
Love changes

VIV
Not mine

LUCIA
I was the more deceived

NOEL and LARRY
Get thee to a nunnery: why wouldst thou be a breeder of sinners ?

NOEL
I am myself indifferent honest; but yet I could accuse me of such things that it were better my mother had not borne me.

LARRY
I am very proud, revengeful, ambitious; with more offences at my back than I have thoughts to put them in, imagination to give them shape, or time to act them in.

VIV
Talk straight

LARRY
What should such fellows as I do crawling between heaven and earth ? We are arrant knaves all; believe none of us.

LARRY and NOEL
Go thy ways to a nunnery.

LUCIA
O ! help him, you sweet heavens !

NOEL
If thou dost marry I'll give thee this plague for thy dowry: be thou as chaste as ice, as pure as snow, thou shalt not escape calumny. Get thee to a nunnery, go; farewell. Or, if thou wilt needs marry, marry a fool; for wise men know well enough what monsters you make of them. To a nunnery, go; and quickly too. Farewell.

LUCIA
O heavenly powers, restore him !

VIV
You'll not get rid of me that easily

NOEL
...
Go to, I'll no more on't; it hath made me mad. I say, we will have no more marriages. To a nunnery, go [EXIT}

VIV
You begrudge what our sex does for me

LARRY
It nearly did for me

VIV
Vicious, aren't you ?
And wrong
You underestimate the power of love
Even your twisted version

LARRY
You promised me we'd make a baby

VIV
NO MORE BLOODY BABIES !
Your sneaky way of eliminating me from the competition
You're not fit to father a child
I know you did your damnedest to block me playing Scarlett O'Hara
Played the baby-card all over Hollywood

LARRY
I tried to stop you making yourself a laughing-stock

VIV
My Scarlett was the greatest female performance of the century

LARRY
Ha !

VIV
Hollywood had you taped
Now you're trying to wreck my career by starving me of love

LARRY
OK you've done your baby-trick
I've done my super-stud trick
Time to move on

VIV
NO !
Our sex is vital
It's not about making babies
It's about making work
I won't let you throw it away
For a rumble with some back-stage whore

LARRY
There's no back-stage whore

VIV
Then why the virginal zip?

LARRY
Because you are smothering me
Because you fill my house with strangers
Because you never sleep
Which means I never sleep

VIV
You sleep
And snore

LARRY
Because of your constant demand for sex
Because of your insatiable need for reassurance

VIV
I give you constant reassurance

LARRY
You are a beautiful talented woman
I love working with you
But you've got to let me breathe
I remember you saying you'd like to eat me
Well you've done it
You've cannibalised me
I have to get to arm's length from you or you'll destroy me

VIV
Who is it ?

LARRY
It's anyone in the wide world who'll have me
But darling... I'm sorry
I can't take any more from you

[VIV attacks him suddenly and violently.
They punch and wrestle.]

VIV
SHIT !
FAITHLESS FUCKING SHIT !
GET OUT !

BOTH
GET OUT OF MY FUCKING LIFE !

LUCIA
O ! what a noble mind is here o'erthrown:
The courtier's, soldier's, scholar's, eye, tongue, sword;
The expectancy and rose of the fair state,
The glass of fashion, and the mould of form,
The observ'd of all observers, quite, quite down !
And I, of all ladies most deject and wretched,
That sucked the honey of his music vows,
Now see that noble and most sovereign reason,
Like sweet bells jangled, out of tune and harsh;
That unmatch'd form and feature of blown youth
Blasted with ecstasy: O ! woe is me,
To see what I have seen, see what I see.

HA HA 8

[VIV will play the following scene extremely light.]

VIV
.....
Where is the beauteous majesty of Denmark ?

LUCIA
How now, Ophelia !

VIV
How should I your true love know
From another one ?
By his cockle hat and staff
And his sandal shoon

LUCIA
Alas ! sweet lady, what imports this song ?

VIV
Say you ? nay, pray you, mark.
He is dead and gone, lady,
He is dead and gone;
At his head a green-grass turf,
At his heels a stone.
O, ho !

LUCIA
Nay, but Ophelia....

VIV
Pray you, mark.
White his shroud as the mountain snow...

LUCIA
Alas ! look here, my lord.

VIV
Larded with sweet flowers;
Which bewept to the grave did go
With true-love showers.

NOEL
How do you, pretty lady ?

VIV
Well, God 'ild you ! They say the owl was a baker's daughter. Lord ! we know what we are, but know not what we may be. God be at your table !

NOEL
Conceit upon her father

VIV
Pray you, let's have no words of this; but when they ask you what it means, say you this :
To-morrow is St Valentine's day,
All in the morning betime,
And I a maid at your window,
To be your Valentine:
Then up he rose, and donn'd his clothes,
And dupp'd the chamber door;

Let in the maid, that out a maid
Never departed more.

NOEL
Pretty Ophelia !

VIV
Indeed, la ! without an oath, I'll make an end on't:
By Gis and by Saint Charity,
Alack, and fie for shame !
Young men will do it, if they come to 't;
By Cock they are to blame..
Quoth she, before you tumbled me,
You promis'd me to wed:
So would I ha' done, by yonder sun,
And thou hadst not come to my bed.

NOEL
How long hath she been thus ?

VIV
I hope all will be well. We must be patient: but I cannot choose but weep, to think they should lay him i' the cold ground. My brother shall know of it: and so I thank you for your good counsel. Come, my coach ! Good-night ladies; good-night, sweet ladies; good-night, good-night.
......
You think I'm stark raving bonkers

LUCIA
We've all been working too hard

NOEL
Come back to Jamaica with me
When we're rested we can start working on *South Sea Bubble*

VIV
You think I'm not good enough to play Shakespeare with Larry

NOEL
I never said that

VIV
For someone who says so much and writes so much
There's an awful lot you don't say

NOEL
My private life's my own affair

VIV
It's part of your public work
It doesn't belong to you

NOEL
I try to make people laugh
Forget that reality is hard and cruel

VIV
I remind them reality is hard and cruel
And may be changed

NOEL
Theatre is essentially entertainment

VIV
Theatre is where we look around corners
At yesterday today and tomorrow

NOEL
You're confusing theatre with the church

VIV
You're confusing it with the bawdy-house

NOEL
For just this once I'll be serious
You're more like me than like Larry
You can make people laugh
You are good sometimes very good in the big tragic roles
But as light commedienne you could be one of the truly great

VIV
You underestimate me
And you underestimate Shakespeare

[SHE will play the following scene extremely dark and disturbingly.]

.....
Where is the beauteous majesty of Denmark ?

LUCIA
How now, Ophelia !

VIV
How should I your true love know
From another one ?
By his cockle hat and staff
And his sandal shoon

LUCIA
Alas ! sweet lady, what imports this song ?

VIV
Say you ? nay, pray you, mark.
He is dead and gone, lady,
He is dead and gone;
At his head a green-grass turf,
At his heels a stone.
O, ho !

LUCIA
Nay, but Ophelia....

VIV
Pray you, mark.
White his shroud as the mountain snow...

LUCIA
Alas ! look here, my lord.

VIV
Larded with sweet flowers;
Which bewept to the grave did go
With true-love showers.

NOEL
How do you, pretty lady ?

VIV
Well, God 'ild you ! They say the owl was a baker's daughter. Lord ! we know what we are, but know not what we may be. God be at your table !

NOEL
Conceit upon her father

VIV
Pray you, let's have no words of this; but when they ask you what it means, say you this :
To-morrow is St Valentine's day,
All in the morning betime,
And I a maid at your window,
To be your Valentine:
Then up he rose, and donn'd his clothes,
And dupp'd the chamber door;
Let in the maid, that out a maid
Never departed more.

NOEL
Pretty Ophelia !

VIV
Indeed, la ! without an oath, I'll make an end on't:
By Gis and by Saint Charity,
Alack, and fie for shame !
Young men will do it, if they come to't;

By Cock they are to blame..
Quoth she, before you tumbled me,
You promis'd me to wed:
So would I ha' done, by yonder sun,
And thou hadst not come to my bed.

NOEL
How long hath she been thus ?

VIV
I hope all will be well. We must be patient: but I cannot choose but weep, to think they should lay him i' the cold ground. My brother shall know of it: and so I thank you for your good counsel. Come, my coach ! Good-night ladies; good-night, sweet ladies; good-night, good-night.

HA HA 9

LUCIA
We met
In that mind-numbing children's play of Basil Dean's
Hannele
I was Third Fairy

NOEL
Aha ! I was Second Fairy so there !

LUCIA
I was only twelve

NOEL
I was a lot older
Going on thirteen
A bit long in the tooth for fairy work
It was my first paid job

LUCIA
Fairies can't be choosers
I had a passionate crush on you

NOEL
So had I

LUCIA
On me ?

NOEL
On me

LUCIA
I never lost it

NOEL
Nor I
I'm pretty good at keeping friends

LUCIA
Apart from disagreeing violently with them about everything

NOEL
I like you shouting and swearing at me

LUCIA
We never fell out 'cos we never fell in

NOEL
To bed ?

LUCIA
One of life's little paradoxes

NOEL
Drummed into me at my mother's knee
'Never go to bed with someone you love !'

LUCIA
Your lovely mother drummed nothing into you but self-belief

NOEL
We're all very positive today
I hope you're not going to borrow money

LUCIA
I borrow from you to reassure myself you still love me

NOEL
I'll always love you

LUCIA
Two hundred quid

NOEL
Sure

LUCIA
No dearest
Just give me a big hug till the end of the month

NOEL
You'll give it back ?

LUCIA
I promise

NOEL
....
....
My mum never learned how to hug
I often wonder how they managed to have children

LUCIA
You were very close

NOEL
Close as 'that' all my life
But not touching
I taught her to hold my hand
When we weren't fighting
……
Like you… she disagreed with me about everything
Argued protested harangued… but never held me back
Every tussle ended in affirmation
A kind of heroic testing
The only thing we agreed on was my High Tory politics

LUCIA
Which is what I really hate about you

NOEL
My legacy from the playing-fields of Teddington
…..
I come from a class on tiptoe to keep their head out of the gutter
The toffs were our gods
We built their ships
Nursed their children
Fought their wars
Aped their manners and their accents
And one in five million of us made it through the class ceiling
And became part of it all
Almost

LUCIA
This year you'll surely get your Special K

NOEL
It's blocked at No. 10
Is it the tax-exile thing ?
Or simply Islington versus Teddington ?
The quality of peer sinks inexorably year on year
It's hardly worth it any more

LUCIA
The monarchy isn't worth it
I see virtue in an honours system

NOEL
The Windsors are wonderful
But unforgiving to young men who fall in love with their princes

LUCIA
A one-way ticket to the tower for you mate
And your prince

NOEL
Actually they're quite ambivalent about me
They still seek me out and invite me to all kinds of tuck-in

LUCIA
You and George were over the top by any standard
I was never so jealous of anything since the Second Fairy

NOEL
Well I can't regret it
It's over
It was real it was wild it was hilarious
And often quite beautiful
Nowadays we might even marry
But I guess the spoilsports would find a way of blocking that
Anyway there'd be one unholy row
Over which of us would wear my mum's white wedding dress

HA HA 10

[VIV forward
LARRY off
LUCIA photographing.]

LARRY [OFF]
My house is full of dossers
There's some fucker passed out in my bed

VIV
It's only Duncan

LARRY [OFF]
What Duncan ?

VIV
The Scottish chap we met at the Savoy

LARRY [OFF]
Get him to hell out of my bed

VIV
Put him in mine

LARRY [OFF]
.....
There's two more in yours

VIV
Duncan's security

……

……

Booze that knocked them out has turned me on
What duffed their wits has fired my head. What ? Hush !

……

It was the midnight train that shrieked. It's gone
Swallowed whole by ravenous night
Open bedrooms mock minders snoring on borrowed time
Pick up the bloody tabs for all if they survive my date-rape spike

LARRY [OFF]
What's that ? Who are you ?

VIV
Shit ! He'll raise the house
Stuck at first base…Hush !
… I left the blades just so…he couldn't miss
I would have done it then but frozen to the spot the moment passed
He looked so like my dad

[Enter LARRY]

My husband !

LARRY
I did it
Did you hear something ?

VIV
I heard the night-train shriek… a raven croak
Did you not speak ?

LARRY
When ?

VIV
Now

LARRY
As I came down ?

VIV
Yes

LARRY
Whisht !
Who's in the other room ?

VIV
Donalbain

LARRY
Look at the mess I'm in !

VIV
What a stupid thing to say,' look at the mess I'm in'

LARRY
The big one laughed in sleep one shouted 'Murther !' waking the other
Me listening they mumbling prayers to sleep

VIV
His brother with him [that is with Donalbain]

LARRY
One cried 'God help me !' the other said 'Amen' as if they saw my butcher's hands
Cusping their fear... I tried to say 'Amen' to his 'God help me'

VIV
It's nothing

LARRY
'Amen' is not a lot to say to ask a blessing
'Amen' stuck in my gorge

VIV
This is no way to talk... It's done
You'll drive us mad

LARRY
A voice in....a voice said 'Sleep no more
Macbeth does murther sleep'
The innocent sleep
Sleep that knits up the ravelled sleave of care
The death of each day's life
Hard labour's bath
Balm of hurt minds
Great nature's second chance
Staple in life's feast

VIV
What are you talking about ?

LARRY
Shouting 'Sleep no more' to all the house
'Glamis has murthered sleep and therefore Cawdor
Shall sleep no more... Macbeth shall sleep no more'

VIV
Are you out of your mind ? There was no such shouting
Get hot water and wash this filth forensic clean and quick about it !
What are these knives doing here you idiot ?
Take them back
Smear blood and gore on the sleeping murtherers

LARRY
Not me !
I don't know what I've done...go back I dare not

VIV
Coward ! Give them here ! It's only meat !
You have the mind of an infant
If there's blood left in him I'll paint a picture that will hang his minders !

[EXIT.
KNOCKING heard.]

LARRY
Who's that ?
Calm now...knocking is knocking
Such hands ... can oceans scour or will they change the colour of the sea ?

[ENTER VIV.]

VIV
Now our hands are colour-matched
If not our hearts [KNOCKING] I hear knocking
Let them wait
A little water makes a wondrous alibi
We'll share a shower
These clothes incinerate
[KNOCKING] More knocking ha ! to wake the dead
Then dress we for the happy mourning day....something casual

LARRY
To know my deed, best not know myself
[KNOCK]
Wake Duncan with thy knocking.. I wish you could
[KNOCK.]

LUCIA
I like it

NOEL [OFF]
There's knocking !

[ENTER NOEL]

Are you all deaf ?

LARRY
We were busy murthering

LUCIA
The knocking came in right on cue

LARRY
....
I prefer the original
Shakespeare's language gives you a bit of distance... like a mask

NOEL
The first time I saw you in *Macbeth*
Everyone was made up to look like masks
It was hilarious
Does my memory serve me right
Or did you all move round like giant puppets ...?

LARRY
Don't !
We called it stylized... it was very fashionable that year

NOEL
I got a fit of the giggles
It got worse and worse the more I....
How does it go ?
'Sleep no more Macbeth [Clump clump clump !]
Glamis has murdered sleep and therefore Cawdor shall sleep no more...'
[Clump clump clump !]

LARRY
You bollox ! I saw you staggering out

NOEL
I had to !

VIV
He needs someone to earth him
I'm his earth-mother

LARRY
Earth-wife

[VIV's voice takes on a harsh violent edge]

VIV
Not any more

LARRY
Sorry ?

LUCIA
They say only lovers should play the Macbeths

LARRY
Excuse me
What do you mean 'not any more' ?

VIV
You speak English ?

LARRY
You are my wife

VIV
We'll see

LARRY
What ?

NOEL
Lucia... maybe we can look at the ....

LUCIA
Shut up Noel

LARRY
We'll see what ?

VIV
....
....

LARRY
You're drunk

VIV
......
......
Larry darling...

LARRY
Yes pet ?

VIV
It's just.....
......
How many times have I told you I loved you ?

LARRY
A million million times......

VIV
And how many times have you told me you loved me ?

LARRY
Two million million times

VIV
It's just...
......
......
I don't love you any more

LUCIA
One second !

LARRY
You really are the cruelest woman

LUCIA
I can't get your eyes

LARRY
I'll shove that camera up your backside !

LUCIA
Gotcha !

VIV
Whatever it was... I think it was a great and real love...
It's finished Larry

LARRY
You're talking about my life

VIV
And mine

HA HA 11

[NOEL dresses as MADAME CARATI, a medium conducting a séance. Lights dim.]

NOEL

Little Jack Horner sat in a corner
Eating a Christmas pie
He stuck in his thumb
And pulled out a plum
Saying 'What a good boy am I...'

....

Nobody there
There's some negative force getting in the way
Oh dearie me...nothing for it but go the whole hog
First the music..........

[A familiar sentimental ballad is played.]

LARRY

Oh please !
Not that tune !

NOEL

The die is cast my friend

LARRY

Madame Carati I beg you...

LUCIA

Don't be ridiculous Charlie !

NOEL

AAAAGH !!

[SHE SCREAMS; falls in a deep trance.]

LUCIA
Madame Carati. are you all right ?

VIV's VOICE
LEAVE HER WHERE SHE IS !

LARRY
Who said that ?

LUCIA
What ?

LARRY
Someone shouted 'Leave her where she is !'

LUCIA
Rubbish

LARRY
It was you

LUCIA
I didn't open my mouth

LARRY
She's a ventriloquist !
Come off it Madame Carati ! We're on to your game !

VIV's VOICE
Good evening Charlie !

LARRY
Who said that ?

LUCIA
You did

LARRY
I didn't open my mouth

LUCIA
That'll be the day !

VIV's VOICE
Charlie dear !
It's been seven years

LARRY
Who is that ?

VIV's VOICE
Don't be silly Charlie
It's Vera

LARRY
Put on the light !
[Light up.]
I've had enough of this chicanery
You may turn it off Madame Carati !
[Light off.]
The game not the light !
[Light up.]

[VERA, dress and skin grey and ghostly, has materialized, unseen by CHARLIE at first.]

I'm going to have a drink.... Ruth ?

LUCIA
No thank you

LARRY
Madame Carati ?

NOEL
[Snore]

LARRY
OH MY GOD IT'S YOU !

VIV
Of course it's me

LARRY
Are you a ghost ?

LUCIA
Are you talking to me ?

VIV
I suppose I am

LARRY
You've been dead seven years

LUCIA
I beg your pardon !

VIV
So this is your latest

LARRY
You two haven't met, have you ?
Ruth this is my first wife, Vera
Vera, this is my present wife, Ruth

VIV
I've been dying to meet you !

LUCIA
Charlie, sit down and stop throwing your drink about

LARRY
Can you not see her ?

LUCIA
Of course I can see her [Madame Carati]

LARRY
Vera

VIV
Yes ?

LUCIA
Who ?

LARRY
Over there

LUCIA
Sit down and have a drop of brandy

LARRY
Why do you keep trying to get me to sit down ?

LUCIA
I want you to relax
You can't relax standing there waving your glass about

VIV
Horses do
Horses sleep standing up

LARRY
I'm not a bloody horse ! [Sits]

LUCIA
No one said you were a horse darling

LARRY
She did

LUCIA
Say when [the brandy]

LARRY
Just now

VIV
I don't think that's wise
He could never hold his drink

LARRY
I'd damn well drink you under the table any time

LUCIA
Of course you would
Drink that up and we'll get you up to bed

VIV
We've a lot of catching-up to do
Get rid of her dear

LARRY
You're nothing but a brazen hussy

LUCIA
I'm not expecting sex, if that's what's worrying you

LARRY
I wasn't talking to you

LUCIA
Neither is Madame Carati I'm sure

LARRY
I was talking to Vera

LUCIA
Oh to hell with Vera

If she's not already there
Go and join her for all I care
I'll be in the spare room if you happen to be interested in saying good-night

VIV
That spare room is the oldest trick in the book

LARRY
Do you have to act the guttersnipe ?

LUCIA
Don't bother then ! [EXIT}

VIV
....
I rather enjoyed that
Like old times

LARRY
I'm hallucinating

VIV
Your grip on reality was always tenuous at best

LARRY
Oh Vera what'll I do ?

VIV
Do what the little woman said... relax

LARRY
Have you come from Heaven or Hell ?

VIV
…….?
You know…. I haven't the faintest idea

LARRY
Any harm asking how long eh you plan to stay ?
You're more than welcome needless to say

VIV
You don't want me back !

LARRY
Nonsense
Though it could be a bit embarrassing… ha ha ha !

VIV
Just needs a bit of flexibility
And you to stop being grumpy and intolerant

LARRY
Was I really grumpy and intolerant ?

VIV
Only when you weren't violent

LARRY
I have such positive memories of our relationship

VIV
You struck me with a billiard-cue
In that awful hotel in Devon

LARRY
Nudged you
You were flirting with a seedy old roué in...

VIV
A teenager... I think he was the village policeman

LARRY
I don't know why you had to come back and....

VIV
You conjured me back
You and Madame Whatsername

LARRY
Well as soon as she wakes up we'll conjure you into your box again
So to speak

VIV
OH OH OH ! You're a horrible man !
I'd like to cry my eyes out

LARRY
Do that dear
Have a good cry

VIV
There's no crying this side of the grave
Oh I do miss it !

LARRY
I'm sorry
You're right of course
I was always grumpy and intolerant
I thought that's what chaps did

VIV
I didn't mind
So long as I believed you loved me

LARRY
I was a bit short on the graces

VIV
You were pretty damn good at some things

LARRY
I was ?
……
What ?

VIV
Never mind

LARRY
……
Can I touch you ?

VIV
Do you want to ?

LARRY
Very much
....
....
Oh dear

VIV
Plenty of time
....
Strangely enough I still have strong sexual feelings towards you

LARRY
Me too

VIV
That doesn't seem fair

LARRY
I loved you with all my heart Vera

VIV
I loved you with all my heart Charlie
.....
Maybe it's just as well we can't touch
....
Relax

LARRY
Mmmmmmm

VIV
Feel anything ?

LARRY
No dear

VIV
You do

LARRY
Only the faintest zephyr of a breeze enfolding me in its warmth…

VIV
Not bad for starters

LARRY
They may lock me in a padded cell
…..
I don't care

VIV
Me neither

LARRY
….
Ruth is waiting in the spare bedroom

VIV
Serves her right

LARRY
Poor Ruth

VIV
To hell with Ruth
....
What do you feel now ?

[LIGHTS DOWN and
suddenly up again
as MADAME CARATI awakes and
springs to her feet.]

NOEL
Aha !

LARRY
Are you all right Madame Carati ?

NOEL
Fit as a top !
Always am after a good trance
.....
Something happened !

VIV
Send her home

LARRY
No

NOEL
Yes it did

LARRY
A great deal happened Madame Carati

NOEL
Where's your wife ?

VIV
I'm here

LARRY
Gone.....

NOEL
OH MY GOD NO NO NO !

LARRY
Gone to bed Madame Carati... she was a little tired

NOEL
Thank heaven for that !
I was afraid we might have vaporized her
[Sniff] Hold ! [Sniff]
I smell ectoplasm

VIV & LARRY
It wasn't me !

NOEL
There is a presence !

I feel my vibrations

LARRY
That's my late wife
Just back from seven years in the grave
Forgive me...
Madame Carati...Vera; Vera... Madame Carati

NOEL
How do you do ?

VIV
I was doing all right till you shoved your nose out

LARRY
She's over there

NOEL
A great pleasure !

LARRY
There !
She moves around quite a bit

NOEL
I take it she is manifesting only to your good self ?

[VERA throws a cushion at Madame CARATI]

VIV
GO AND FUCK YOURSELF YOU GREASY HARIDAN !

NOEL
Splendid !
She's trying to make contact with me !

LARRY
I believe she's a little upset at being interrupted when we were ..eh...

NOEL
Perfectly natural
Or supernatural. Ha ha ha !
Oh this is splendid! Really beyond my wildest expectations
Here I must confess that heretofore I have never been fortunate enough to manage a marital re-union
There appears to be significant resistance to the idea from both sides of the divide
.....
May I ask if your late wife appears to be ..eh... complete ?

VIV
A damn sight more complete than you !

LARRY
I was in the process of checking that when you...

NOEL
Excellent !
Perhaps I can assist

VIV
If you lay a finger on me
You randy old dyke

I'll tear you limb from bloody limb !

LARRY
Vera is shy almost to a fault

VIV
HAVE YOU NO HOME TO GO TO
YOU STINKING TART?

LARRY
She is just saying how much she admired your work from the other side

NOEL
Too very kind
One does what one can

VIV
Well you can do us all a favour
And get yourself on to your broomstick goodnight !

LARRY
My late wife is enquiring whether you can now assist her to return to……

VIV
BRUTE !
I'm barely in through the wall
And you're trying to get rid of me !
Well I'll not bloody go without a fight !
GET OUT ! GET OUT !

[Belays MADAME CARATI with
a cushion]

NOEL
Wonderful !
She's trying to play with me ! Ha ! Ha ! Ha !

[MADAME CARATI joins the
game, making wild cushion-blows at thin air.]

VIV
OUT OF MY HOUSE YOU BITCH !
OUT ! OUT !

LARRY
VERA ! MADAME CARATI !
PLEASE CONTROL YOURSELVES !

NOEL
THIS IS STUPENDOUS STUFF !
HAVEN'T HAD SUCH FUN SINCE THE [MAIDENHEAD]
POLTHERGEISTS !
HA ! GOT YOU DIDN'T I ?

LARRY
VERA !
MADAME !

[GENERAL MAYHEM AND WRESTLING
taking CHARLIE and MADAME CARATI into a
most compromising position when RUTH enters.]

LUCIA
CHARLES !

MADAME CARATI !
WHAT IN THE NAME OF GOD IS GOING ON ?

……….

……….
Hold it there one second ! [Camera]

NOEL
Oh dear !
I do enjoy a bit of the old slap and tickle…

VIV
Obviously

LARRY
I hope they're not for the *News Of The World*

LUCIA
Would you mind ?

LARRY & NOEL
Yes I would !

LUCIA
That's all right then
Your dark secret is safe with me !

[Light change. The actors start to lose their grip on their lines and other realities. The set collapses. The performance ends in controlled anarchy.]

VIV
There are no secrets in this house
.....
At least that was my understanding of the arrangements

[CAST combine to sing us out with
BAD TIMES ARE RIGHT AROUND THE CORNER]

CAST (sing)
Mountbatten down the hatches
In Which We Served the war
One can't knight Coward
He's far too for'ard
And the Duke of Kent is just a queen too far

With Viv our sleepless diva
You're pushing at an open door
Stray cats or fellas
With raised umbrellas
Bring 'em in she's already coming back for more

The world recalls Sir Larry's
Hamlet and Henry Five
Unhappy knight
[Viv: 'The man's a shite !']
Our famous lovers stand knife to knife

Olé! Olé! Olé!
Bad times are here to stay

Refrain:

Bad times are right around the corner
Good times a pipe-dream from the past
Folk like Viv and Larry
Should never ever marry
Or not expect it, if they do, to last
So let's scowl and frown
With spirits down
Wallow in self-pity for us poor old rich
Lay out your troubles and dump the bag
Life is such a bloody bitch !

END

www.ingramcontent.com/pod-product-compliance
Ingram Content Group UK Ltd.
Pitfield, Milton Keynes, MK11 3LW, UK
UKHW012237240726
13966UKWH00003B/1137